Feeding Time

Elspeth Graham

Illustrated by John Bendall-Brunello

FAMILY LEARNING

It was time for Stan
to feed the animals.

Stan had some fish.

"These fish are for you,"
he said.

Stan had some bananas.

"These bananas are for you," he said.

Stan had some bones.

"These bones are for you,"
he said.

Stan had some nuts
for the birds.

He had some carrots for
the rabbits.

"What do I have for you?"
said Stan.

Stan looked and looked
but he had no ants.

The ants had run away.

"What are we going to do?" said Stan.

"Have some of my food!"
said Stan.

Picture Words

fish

banana

bone

nuts

carrot

bird

rabbit

ant

food